The little

**Books should be returned on or before the
last date stamped below.**

The Canterbury tales

The Little Brother's Tale

MARGARET RYAN

Illustrated by Adrian Reynolds

Hodder
Children's
Books

A division of Hodder Headline plc

Text copyright © Margaret Ryan 1998
Illustrations copyright © Adrian Reynolds 1998

The right of Margaret Ryan to be identified as
the Author of the Work have been asserted by her
in accordance with the Copyright, Designs and Patents
Act 1998

This edition first published
by Hodder Children's Books in 1998

10 9 8 7 6 5 4 3 2

ISBN 0340 714514

Printed and bound in Great Britain by
Mackays of Chatham plc, Chatham, Kent

Hodder Children's Books
A division of Hodder Headline plc
338 Euston Road
London NW1 3BH

For Iain, with love

Chapter One

One day Mum asked me if I'd like a little sister.

"No," I said. "I've got a big sister and that's bad enough." Bossy Boots Canterbury should be her name, not Kate.

Then I thought about it. A little
sister would be smaller than
me. I could boss her about.

"Okay," I said to Mum. "I'd
like a little sister, so long as she
doesn't want the top bunk in
my room, and
doesn't mess
around with
my dinosaur."

"That won't be a problem," said Mum. "Not for a while, anyway."

And for a while it wasn't.

When the baby arrived she was really ugly. All red and wrinkled like a dried up plum.

"She looks just like you, Tom," said Great Aunt Izzy.

"Like ME?" I screeched. "Time to get new glasses, Auntie."

Mum gave me a row for being rude.

Mum and Dad called the baby Anastasia. Annie for short. I called her Baldy because she had no hair. No hair and no teeth. She looked exactly like my Grandad when he goes to bed at night.

But Baldy got lots of presents. Mostly boring cuddly toys which Kate pinched. There wasn't a computer game in sight. Not even a football. She did get a jingly pink ball that hung over her cot, though. I used to thump it whenever I went past. It always woke her up and made her yell.

It was great till one day Mum found out and nearly thumped *me*. Babies are no fun at all.

And their table manners are disgusting. As soon as the baby could eat her pudding from a plate she decided to wear the plate on her head.

"Nice one, Baldy. Yellow custard looks good dribbling down your nose, especially mixed with green snot. YUK!"

One lunchtime, while Mum was in the garden hanging out some washing, I gave Baldy a bit of my hamburger. It was covered in tomato ketchup and was super delicious. Baldy loved it.

Gummed it all down. Then
she was sick over everything.
Mum came in and thought the
tomato ketchup was blood.
She phoned the doctor before
I had a chance to explain.

The doctor arrived, sniffed
at the baby, and said…

"This blood is tomato
ketchup, Mrs Canterbury."

Mum turned white,
then red.

I was sent to my
room in disgrace.

Then Dad came in and said,
"You're a disgrace, Tom
Canterbury, and so is your
room. Tidy it up right now."

Then Kate came in and said,
"Imagine feeding
the baby
hamburger
covered in
ketchup.
What an idiot!"

I crept downstairs later when they were all watching telly.

"Look," I said. "I was only trying to help. Baby food looks horrible. How can you expect Baldy to grow up to play football if all she ever gets is slops?"

But they just didn't understand about the hamburger.

And it got worse.

Chapter Two

A while after that, one Sunday afternoon, I was sitting quietly at the kitchen table, glueing the horns on to my triceratops when…

DISASTER STRUCK!

Mum's cousin Daisy arrived.
Daisy's a BIG lady. BIG hands,
BIG feet, BIG everything.

I don't think she should be
called after a little flower.
I think she should be called
after a BIG tree. Like a HUGE
oak or a GIANT pine. I had
already mentioned this to
Mum, who told me not to be
cheeky. Anyway Daisy had
BIG news.

"I'm getting married to
Martin," she said.

"How
wonderful!"
said Mum.

"That's nice,"
said Dad.

19

"And I'd like Kate and Tom
to be flower girl and page boy
at the wedding."

"Really?"
gasped Kate.

"Forget it!"
I squeaked.

"Don't be silly, Tom," said
Mum. "You'll love it. You'll
have a great time."

And she gave me one of her
steely-eyed looks. The kind
that says:
"Be quiet
or you're in
for it later."

So I shut up, but I put on my horrible face. I know it's horrible because I've practised it in the mirror. I went on with my model and pretended I wasn't listening, but I was.

Kate had to wear a long frilly dress and a flowery thing on her head for the wedding. She was delighted.

I was to wear a velvet suit and a frilly shirt. I was disgusted.

I immediately decided to run away from home, run away to sea, or at least to my grandad's round the corner.

I had seen men
in velvet suits
on the covers
of Mum's
old Abba
records. YUK!

But there was no way out.
I checked with Grandad and
he agreed.

"Looks like you'll have to go through with it, Tom. Sometimes a boy's got to do what a boy's got to do."

Then the shopping began.

We went to a really posh shop
and soon Kate was prancing
about in a flowery peach and
white frilly dress. She twirled
round and round in it.

"How do I look?" she said.

"Like Grandad's window box," I said.

Then she stuck a matching flowery thing on her head.

"How do I look now?" she said.

"Like a stupid window box."
She flounced off in a huff.

Then it was my turn to get dressed up.

The shop lady, who smelled of moth balls, brought out a grey velvet suit, and tried it on me.

"How does it feel, dear?" she asked.

"Like I'm wearing Great Aunt Izzy's cat," I said.

The shop lady was *not* pleased. Neither was my Mum.

Kate sighed loudly.

"Little brothers," she said, "are such a pain."

I hate it whens she acts like she's so grown up, so I yanked her pigtail.

She yelled and that set
Baldy off.

Mum's face got
very red and
we left the shop
quickly.

When we got home I was
sent to my room in disgrace
again. I didn't care. That suit
was horrible.

But I got it in the end. Mum
and Dad had a severe word
with me. Kate had a severe
word with me. Even Baldy. I
think her word was Babba, or
maybe it was Abba. And that
was before she had seen me
in the suit!

I hung the suit at the back
of my wardrobe. Correction,
Mum hung the suit at the back

of my wardrobe. I had flung it
on the floor and walked across
it. Several times!

Chapter Three

"You should learn to look after your clothes, Tom," said Kate, hanging up her new High School uniform in her wardrobe. "Then you wouldn't look so scruffy."

"I don't look scruffy," I said.
"I'm in the latest fashion."
And I was.

Holey jeans,
holey T-shirt,
holey
trainers.

Actually, the trainers were past it, and I'd seen a brilliant new pair in a sports shop in the High Street.

"Could you buy me new trainers, Mum?" I asked. "These ones are falling apart."

"Sorry, Tom," said Mum, "you'll have to wait. Now that Annie has learned to walk I need to buy her proper shoes and Kate needs new shoes to start the High School."

"But what about me?" I said. "My friends'll laugh at me in these old trainers."

"Sorry," said Mum, "but they'll have to do. After the wedding you can wear the new shoes we bought you for that."

She had to be joking. The new shoes were black shiny patent leather with big buckles.

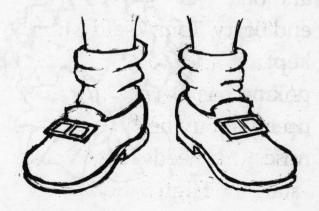

I just hoped everyone would
be too busy laughing at the
velvet suit to look at my feet.
Perhaps if I took small quick
steps no one would notice. But
I knew they would because
the other thing about the new
shoes was that they squeaked.

The final straw was the
big peach velvet bow tie. It
wouldn't sit straight round
my neck,
and one
end of it
kept
poking
up my
nose.

But Mum said it looked fine,
and made me try the whole
outfit on to let cousin
Daisy see.

"Oh, how lovely," said Daisy.

"Have you left your guide dog outside today?" I muttered.

"Go to your room, Tom, and don't be so rude," said Mum.

I've been spending a lot of time in my room recently. I don't know why. I get the blame for everything. It's not fair.

Chapter Four

The day of the wedding
wasn't fair either. It poured
down.

"Oh dear," said Mum.
"Annie's new
floppy hat
will get wet."

"And my
new dress
will get wet,"
wailed Kate.

I went and stood out in the
rain. Maybe the velvet suit
would get wet and shrink and
I could go to the wedding in
my T-shirt and Bermudas.

But Mum pulled me
indoors quickly.

"Don't be so silly, Tom," she said.

"Do try to grow up, Tom," sniffed Kate.

"Abba babba," said Baldy.

Then Dad was called in to get ready for the wedding. He'd been underneath the car fixing an oil leak. I *had* offered to help him.

"No," said Mum. "You'll get your velvet suit dirty."

That was the idea.

Soon it was time to pile into the car and go to the wedding. Mum and Dad sat in the front. Kate and I sat in the back with Baldy in between us in her car

seat. She chewed on her new
hat till it was really soggy, then
hit me with it all the way to
the church. Kate sat all prim
and proper, hardly daring to
move in case she messed her

hair or creased her dress. I
played with my suit. If you
rub velvet the wrong way you
can make it look a darker
colour. So I had one pale grey
arm and one dark grey arm.

43

I was just starting on my left
leg when I saw it. An oily rag.
Dad must have left it on the
floor when he
was fixing
the leak.

"Oh dear," I thought.
"How untidy."

And, being a very tidy
person, I picked it up. Now I
had oily hands. Oops! I was
just about to wipe them on my
trousers when the car stopped.
We had arrived at the church.
I dropped the rag and
scrunched my hands into fists
so the black oily bits wouldn't
show. And they didn't. Not
until I picked up the huge

white train on cousin Daisy's
huge white frock.

I tried to rub the black bits
off with my sleeve but that
just made it worse.

"Stop that," hissed Kate.
I thought she said 'drop
that' and I let the train go.
Right into a muddy puddle.

That's when everyone saw the two oily hand marks. They looked just like the hand print pictures we used to do in school. I thought they looked quite nice, but nobody else did.

Then there was the wedding service. It went on for ages. Kate listened to every word and sang all the hymns at the top of her voice. Baldy went 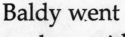 to sleep with her plug in.

I got bored so I made rabbit's ears out of my hanky just like Grandad had shown me. Dad glared at me. So I picked my nose.

Mum glared at me. So I
whistled along with a hymn.
Kate glared at me. What was
I to do to pass the time?
Inspiration! I squeaked my
shoes. Just a little bit. Just to
see how it sounded. It sounded
loud. Very loud. And just when

the bride and groom were
saying 'I do', as well.

Everyone glared at me, so
I yelled "MOUSE, MOUSE",
and all the old ladies jumped
up on their pews and
screamed. Kate jumped up
too and ripped her new dress.

Baldy woke up and started to yell. The bride and groom were NOT pleased. They told Mum later they would NEVER EVER have any children of their own in case they turned out like me.

But, apart from that, everything went well.

Until the reception.

Chapter Five

The reception was in a big fancy hotel.

"When do we get to eat?" I asked Mum. "I'm starving."

"Soon," she said. "There's a toast first."

"Toast? Good, I like toast. I hope there's strawberry jam with it – or ketchup."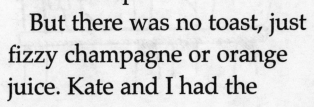

But there was no toast, just fizzy champagne or orange juice. Kate and I had the orange juice. Mum and Dad had the champagne. Mum said champagne always made her sleepy, so when she wasn't looking I gave some of hers to Baldy. It worked well. She went to sleep. Once she'd stopped hiccuping.

Eventually we sat down to eat. It was all fancy food and salads. Not a hamburger or a bottle of ketchup in sight. I had some pink fishy stuff which I didn't like so I leaned over the high chair and gave it to Baldy.

She didn't like it either. She gave a great big hiccup and sicked it up all over herself and Kate. Kate screamed and tried to get the sick out of the flowery thing in her hair. Just to be helpful, I took my spoon and scraped the sick off Baldy's dress and offered it to her again. Sometimes she'll eat things second time round.

Kate said she'd never been so embarrassed in all her life.

But that was before I ruined the wedding cake.

I didn't *mean* to ruin it, because it looked very nice. Tasted nice too. I'd sneaked a bit of icing off it 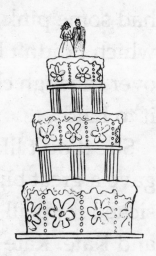 earlier when I was starving.

The bride and groom had cut the cake, and the waiter had come to take it away to be sliced up into little bits, when I discovered the one good thing about my new shoes.

They were great for sliding in,
and the hotel had a beautiful
polished dance floor.

I decided it was time to
practise for the Olympic
Sliding Championships.

"Wheeeeeeeeee…" I went,
across the floor.

"Boof," I went, into the
waiter carrying the cake.

"Thud," went the cake on to the floor and broke into a million pieces.

So, later on, we didn't get
one bit of cake each. We got
lots of bits. Little crumbly bits.
I picked out all the best bits
with icing on.

Then Mum phoned Grandad
and asked him to come and
take me away.

I didn't want to go. By then
I was having a great time,
sliding in and out among
the dancers.

I didn't mean to knock down
the two old ladies.

But Grandad came to fetch me.
"He's been a pest," Mum said
to Grandad. "When you get
home, send him straight
to his room."

Grandad nodded, but when we got home we had fish and chips out of the paper and watched the telly instead.

"When you were little, Grandad," I asked him between bites, "were you always in trouble like me?"

"Oh yes," said Grandad. "Like you, I was stuck in the middle of the family. My big brother and my little sister always seemed to manage to get away with everything, but I always got caught."

"So what did you do, Grandad?"

"Learned *not* to get caught."

"Could you teach *me* not to get caught, Grandad?"

"I could," said Grandad. And he did…

If you enjoyed reading this Canterbury Tales story, look out for book 1...

THE CANTERBURY TALES
The Big Sister's Tale

Margaret Ryan

One day Mum asked me if I'd like a little brother.
"No," I said. "I'd rather have a pony."
But a few months later I got a little brother anyway.

Kate's never been a big sister before. And she's not sure she wants to start now.

As Tom grows up, everybody thinks he's sweet - except Kate. Perhaps the family holiday is the time to put him in his place?

If you enjoyed reading this Canterbury Tales story, look out for book 3...

THE CANTERBURY TALES
The Little Sister's Tale

Margaret Ryan

No one asked me if I'd like a big brother or a big sister.

Kate and Tom were already part of the Canterbury family when I was born, so I was stuck with them...

Annie doesn't think it's fair being the youngest.

She gets Kate's old clothes and Tom's old toys.

She even has to share her bedroom.

But Annie's got an idea - and this time she's going to get her own way!